RĀJO and RĀJA

by Lisa Dass

Illustrated by Mrinal Mitra

LONGMAN

RAJO and RAJA

From her position at the top of the mango tree, Rajo could see the land stretching away over the high walls and wrought iron gate that bordered her garden.

Rajo gazed past the long tree-lined lanes with large flat-roofed houses belonging to her neighbours, all the way to Bombay itself. The gleaming city was shimmering in the haze of the midday sun.

Rajo loved to climb this particular tree and look out at the city – the city where her parents both worked as famous and glamorous film stars. She and her twin brother, Raja, were hardly ever allowed to go to Bombay in case they were mobbed by her parents' adoring fans.

How Rajo wished that her parents were not rich, but were simple farmers instead. Then perhaps she would be free – free to run in the streets with other children, free to romp and jump and play, free to climb trees without being scolded by the maids for ruining expensive clothes ... free to have fun.

Rajo hated being confined in her expensive house with cooks, maids, tutors and her boring brother, Raja. Raja didn't seem to mind that he wasn't allowed out. He spent all his time sitting in his room with his head stuck in some scientific magazine or other.

When Raja wasn't reading he was tinkering with any piece of machinery that he could lay his hands on, from the TV set to his mother's hair-dryer or the brand new alarm clock that Rajo had received as a present. Rajo had been furious when she found out and had lashed out at Raja until Roshanlal, the house boy, had forced them apart. Raja had pleaded that the clock was a vital component of his new "sonic dog screecher", but Rajo ignored him. Since then, Rajo had taken the alarm clock and stormed off to her special tree.

At that moment something caught her attention. A procession of sleek black limousines wound its way up the hill towards their gates. From the gold crest on the bonnet, Rajo recognised the first car as her parents', but she was curious about the others.

The cars swung through the open gates, crunched up the sandy driveway and ground to a halt outside the massive verandah of the house. The car doors were promptly opened by a red-turbaned doorman. Out stepped four young girls dressed in frilly pastel dresses· edged with lace and ribbons.

"Oh no," Rajo groaned from her lofty perch, "not the cousins!"

She would have to come down now, she knew it, but she would hold out until the very last minute.

Rajo watched the four petite figures step daintily onto the verandah as Raja was brought out to meet them. Shyly, each girl tied a brightly coloured band of cotton onto his wrist before whispering something to him. Then they moved into a corner and dissolved into a fit of nervous giggles.

"Oh no!" Rajo groaned again. "It's *Raksha Bandan**, I'd forgotten. I can't believe that those prissy girls have come here to do THAT!"

"RAJO," her maid called from the foot of the tree, "you are to come down this instant."

Rajo hesitated, she didn't want to go down.

"Come on."

Rajo sighed. Life just wasn't fair.

"Good grief! Look at the state of you!" The maid shrieked as she tried to remove the clumps of dried leaves and twigs that had attached themselves to Rajo's hair and clothes.

"Leave me alone," Rajo said crossly,

*Raksha: protection
Bandan: to tie
Raksha Bandan is a Hindu festival

stomping off in the direction of the verandah. Today was not turning out to be a good day. Exactly how bad a day it was to be, Rajo was about to find out.

"Ah Rajo, you have come at last..." her mother broke off to look in horror at her daughter's grubby condition. "Er... your cousins are here."

"I know!" Rajo glued her eyes sullenly to the floor. She felt awkward with her long gangly arms and muscular legs formed from years of running around the gardens. She felt out of place here with her elegant parents, her dainty cousins and her useless brother.

"Rajo," her mother persisted, "it is Raksha Bandan today. Have you made a *Rakhi** for your brother?"

Rajo shook her head.

"I thought as much..." said her mother knowingly, "... so I've got an extra one here for you."

"Rats," Rajo muttered as her mother put the strip of bright red cotton firmly in her hand.

"Go and tie it on Raja and ask his protection for the coming year."

It was more than Rajo could bear.

Rakhi: fancy string band

"No!" she shrieked. "No I won't!"

"What do you mean?" her father said.

"I won't tie a Rakhi on him, and I won't ask for his protection. Why should I? He couldn't protect me from a fly. When he lost his magnifying glass he cried like a baby. I didn't even cry when that cricket ball hit me on the shins."

Rajo flung the band onto the shiny verandah floor, where it slithered to a stop under a chair beside Raja.

"Tell HIM to put that on ME, because I'm not going to put it on a wimp."

Fighting back hot tears of anger Rajo turned, jumped down the verandah steps, two at a time, and fled into the farthest corner of the garden. She ran straight to a crumbling part of the wall that was just low enough for her to climb over, to escape.

Back on the verandah, several sets of open mouths watched Rajo's disappearing back, until her father came to his senses and snapped his shut. Rajo had gone too far this time.

"Go after her Raja," he commanded.

"But... I..." the young boy stammered. He hated having to chase his twin sister.

"Go on," his father urged.

Raja set off at a slow lollop across the lush lawns. He knew which tree Rajo liked to climb – although he hoped that she hadn't gone there because he hated heights. No... the branches were deserted.

Raja looked behind the banana trees, on top of the gate house roof and ended up skirting the wall that closed in their garden from the outside world. It was then that he came across the crumbling gap. Perhaps it was because he and Rajo were twins that they had the same eye for detail, for he too saw the way out, hidden deep behind a tangled mass of creepers. It was because they were twins that Raja knew beyond a shadow of a doubt that his sister had gone over that wall. He could also guess where she would be heading – to the lake.

What should he do? Return and tell his father? But then Rajo would be in terrible trouble for going out of the compound alone. No, it would be much better if he slipped out quietly and persuaded her to come back. No one would be any the wiser.

Raja scrambled over the loose bricks and made his way through the sunshine and down to the lake. Sure enough, there he found Rajo sitting defiantly on a red, sandy bank. Without looking up, Rajo said,

"If you've come to make me tie that thing on you you can think again, you wimp."

Raja plumped himself down beside his sister. "Don't call me a wimp," Raja implored. "It isn't my fault. Actually if you really want to know, Rakhis make me feel like a girl."

"What's wrong with being a girl?"

"Nothing, nothing. I just feel silly with bangles."

Rajo smiled.

"So do I sometimes."

For a while they both stared silently at the sluggish brown water. Rajo looked at her brother. He was all right now and again.

"I think that we'd better be heading back before they find out that we're not in the garden," Raja suggested.

"All right then."

The twins stood up. They had only gone a few steps back, towards the dusty road, when a

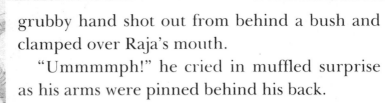

grubby hand shot out from behind a bush and clamped over Raja's mouth.

"Ummmmph!" he cried in muffled surprise as his arms were pinned behind his back.

Rajo whirled around to see two skinny men advancing on her. One of them caught hold of her hand.

Rajo jerked it violently and the man fell off balance. The other man approached warily. Rajo hunched herself into a karate position ready to kick him if he came too close... which he did. The man fell back in pain, clutching a sore shin.

By this time the first man had got up and was tackling Rajo from behind. He had hold of her

17

around the waist and Rajo was punching and kicking him for all she was worth, but it was no good. The second man hobbled angrily over on his bad leg and tied Rajo's arms firmly behind her back. Raja looked at his sister in despair as she was pulled, red-faced, into a nearby car. The captives were taken to an old deserted building nearby. There they were pushed down some steps into an evil smelling basement and thrown inside. The key grated in the lock.

Fortunately, because she had been struggling so much, Rajo's bonds had not been tied very tightly. She wriggled and squirmed frantically until her hands were free. Then she undid all the others.

As soon as the gag was off her mouth, she shouted angrily,

"You fool Raja! Why didn't you stop them? I nearly had mine."

"You are the fool," her brother answered, as soon as Rajo undid his gag. "It's your fault that we were outside the garden in the first place. You never do as you are told. Now we are in big trouble."

"But you didn't fight, you didn't do any

'protecting' did you?"

"How could I with my hands behind my back! Look, this is not the time to argue, we have to get out of here. They will be demanding a ransom from Mummy and Daddy."

Rajo quietened at that sobering thought. She could picture the headlines, 'BABU'S AND BIBI'S CHILDREN KIDNAPPED'.

"They will have to pay a fortune to get us back," Rajo said.

"What do we do now?"

"We have to get out, that's what we do."

For the next half an hour the twins hatched a plot – one that should at least get them out of the gloomy basement.

They decided to stretch Rajo's *chunnih** across the door as a trip wire, but the main problem was that they needed to attract the guards' attention.

"Maybe we could shout," Rajo suggested. So each twin took an end of the chunnih at either side of the door and yelled themselves hoarse. Rajo was rather good at that, but the walls of the basement were so thick that even she could not make the guard hear.

*chunnih: scarf

"We need something to make a really loud noise," Raja muttered.

He rooted around in his pockets and produced a lumpy metal object. Totally absorbed, he began twiddling with the connections.

"What is it?" Rajo asked.

"It's the sonic dog screecher, but I'm not sure that it's going to be any use. The noise is very high pitched, amplified through this speaker here, but it's only audible to dogs not humans."

"Oh that's fabulous, now we'll have a dog patrol looking out for us!" Rajo said irritably.

"If only I had your alarm clock, then I could rig the alarm sound through the amplifier instead."

"But I've got it! Here, it's in my pocket."

A delighted Raja took the clock and began undoing the back.

"When this goes off it will make enough noise to wake the gods."

Ten minutes of careful adjustments later, the alarm was set. The clock rang with an ear-splitting noise that made the twins cringe, but they managed to hold the chunnih steady.

The guard who rushed in fell flat on his face.

With a blood curdling scream, Rajo jumped on top of the man and pinned his arms back in an arm lock.

"Quick," she cried, "tie him up, Raja."

Using the ropes that they themselves had been tied up with, the twins bound and gagged the guard. Then, being careful not to make any more noise, they shut him in the dingy basement.

"Shh... we must be careful now," Rajo whispered. "There are two more."

The other two men, however, were not to be found and the doors and shutters of the house were all firmly locked. The twins moved through dusty rooms full of empty beer bottles and what appeared to be strange digging machines. They were out of the basement, but still trapped in the house.

"Let's go and torture the guard until he tells us the way out," Rajo suggested.

But the twins didn't need to do that, for on their way back to the basement, they came across an opening in the wall. It was like a large rabbit burrow.

"A secret tunnel," Rajo hissed. "I bet that's

the way out, come on."

Finding a stump of candle, Rajo lit it and started to climb down into the yawning blackness.

"But… but… it's dark," stammered Raja nervously. "I can't go in there."

"Well shut your eyes, then you won't see it," Rajo suggested helpfully.

"How will I know where to go?"

"Listen I've got an idea. Take off those Rakhis and give them to me."

Raja did as his sister asked. Deftly Rajo undid them and re-knotted them into a long thread.

"Here," she said. "You hold that end and I'll hold this one. Now you can close your eyes and you still won't get lost."

Raja agreed reluctantly and stepped timidly into the gaping nothingness. His heart was thudding so loudly that he was sure the whole of Bombay would think that an earthquake was coming. Eerie shadows from the candle danced monster-like on the narrow tunnel walls. But never once did Raja scream; with eyes shut tight, he clung onto the Rakhi bands like a drowning boy to a life belt.

After what seemed like days, but was probably only twenty minutes, the tunnel ended and the children emerged from the earthy dampness behind a bush in their very own garden. Up beyond the slope stood their house and, on the verandah, the twins could make out the figures of their parents and the other two kidnappers!

"I'll bet they're handing over the ransom right now," Raja hissed.

"Let's go and stop them!"

"No wait," said Rajo. "I've got a better plan."

She whispered in his ear and, smiling, Raja nodded.

The twins crept stealthily up the garden, taking care not to make any noise. On the way, they each picked up a good sized stick. When they were at the foot of the verandah, Rajo gave the signal and the children ran up the steps. They jabbed their sticks into the backs of the crooks – just as their sobbing mother was handing over her famous jewels.

"Drop them!" Rajo commanded fiercely. "This is a hold up. Put your hands up, both of you."

Raja thought that his sister overdid the gangster part, but then she <u>was</u> the daughter of film stars and it did have the desired effect of making the kidnappers shoot their hands straight up in the air!

Immediately, their mother rushed to hug the twins, but Rajo shot a warning look at the sticks and said, "Perhaps someone should phone the police and have these crooks put away."

Her mother understood at once and went to the telephone.

Later that evening, when all the police questioning and tears of joy were over, Rajo and Raja sat beside their parents on the shady verandah breathing the sweet-scented night air.

"You know," said their father, "those men were digging a tunnel here to rob us. It was only by chance that they saw you and decided that they might get more money from a ransom."

"Ugh..." shuddered their mother, "we could all have been murdered in our beds."

"No chance of that now, the police are going to fill the tunnel in tomorrow."

Rajo was secretly disappointed about that; she had been looking forward to having an easy method of escaping from the garden, should she ever need it!

"Which reminds me," continued her father sternly, "you two should not have been out of the compound in the first place." The twins hung their heads.

"Well..." Rajo muttered, "you shouldn't have tried to make me put a Rakhi on him."

"No," added Raja, "after all, it was Rajo who protected me in the tunnel. I wouldn't have made it back otherwise. I should put one on her."

With that he slipped off a shiny yellow band and tied it firmly around his sister's wrist.

"Actually you were the one with the dog whistle that raised the alarm," Rajo admitted. "If it hadn't been for that we might still be in that poky dungeon now. Maybe I will put one on you after all."

Rajo spotted the red Rakhi that had lain, unnoticed, on the floor since that morning. Slowly she tied it around Raja's wrist.

"It was your alarm clock, though."

"That's teamwork."

Rajo took her brother's hand and raised it up. Together they chorused,

"We'll protect each other!"

The NASTY NEIGHBOUR

The house looked hungry for someone to live in it. It stood, red bricked and straight, in the street – next to the end of the terrace. Reeta and Vijay looked up at their tall new home with delight. Although the paintwork was peeling off, the children could

see that the house looked proud. It had been empty for two years before the Chopra family had decided to buy it.

Reeta and Vijay fell in love with it at first sight. The children loved the steep, narrow staircases. They loved the loud echoing bedrooms with their high, ornate ceilings and the long landings on different levels. The whole place was so much more exciting than the tiny flat that they had been used to. Best of all, though, the children loved having a garden.

Actually it wasn't much of a garden, more of a yard really, paved over with pink and grey concrete patio slabs. Reeta was disappointed about this because she would have liked a proper garden. Still, at least they had somewhere to play outside now. Reeta even discovered a little strip of soil running along the bottom of a fence and, although it wasn't much, she could probably manage to grow some sweet peas there.

At the bottom of the garden stood a small flat-roofed shed and, from the top, Reeta and Vijay had a bird's eye view of all the back gardens in the terrace. Most of the gardens, as far as the eye could see, were covered with lawns surrounded by manicured flower beds. However, the garden which interested Reeta most was the one right next door, the garden belonging to Mr Shelley.

Reeta and Vijay met Mr Shelley the first time they climbed up onto the shed roof. Reeta couldn't help but stare at the garden, for every available inch was crammed, jungle-like. A small greenhouse bulged with different plants and flowers and the rest of the garden was filled with gooseberry and blackcurrant bushes and every variety of plant imaginable. It was a gardener's paradise.

"Why couldn't we have moved to a place with a garden like that?" Reeta drooled enviously.

Just then, a bent figure with a balding head and bushy white moustache appeared from the back door and began to shuffle down the central path. The old man was dressed in baggy brown trousers and a shapeless tweed jacket, with trowels and forks poking out of his pockets.

The man stopped abruptly in his tracks. He paused to sniff the air, then, almost as though he could smell children, he lifted his head and

stared at Reeta and Vijay perched on the shed roof like birds.

"Good afternoon," Vijay began.

"Gerroff! Get out of here!" the old man yelled angrily.

The two children sat still in stunned silence.

"Go away you nosey parkers!"

The old man raised his fist.

"Can't you foreigners speak English? GO!"

Without wasting any time, Reeta and Vijay scrambled back down into their own garden. In his haste, Vijay scraped his knee on the rough sides of the shed.

"Yeouch!" he cried, as his knee began to throb and a thin trickle of blood oozed out onto the concrete.

"Wasn't he rude?" said Reeta helping Vijay up. "I didn't think that he would mind us looking at his garden – after all, we weren't touching anything."

A few days later, the Chopra family were all together in the living room. Mrs Chopra was helping Vijay to make some colourful candles ready for the coming Diwali celebrations. As the autumn weather had turned chilly, Mr Chopra was coaxing a blaze out of the freshly made fire.

Crouched on the floor, in front of the fire, Reeta practised on her sitar. With the long finger board resting on her shoulder, Reeta's fingers moved skillfully up and down the strings. Mr Chopra was well-known as a sitar player and he was often asked to perform at parties and weddings. Reeta gently stroked the thick strings and a beautiful tune floated out. It was a song about the gods Rama and Sita that her father had taught her. She was practising it to play for the guests who would be coming for Diwali.

Reeta was only half way through the first verse when there came a thunderous thumping from the wall, making her fingers jump from the finger board.

"Mr Shelley must be hanging some pictures," Mrs Chopra said, patting molten wax into little containers.

Reeta paused in her playing and the thumping stopped. Frowning with concentration, Reeta read the music and decided to start the song again from the beginning. No sooner had she reached the chorus than the banging started again. This time it was much nearer and louder, it was on their front door.

Mrs Chopra stood up and patted her bun into place before answering the door. Outside stood their next door neighbour.

"Why hello Mr Shelley," she said in her softly lilting voice.

"Won't you come in?"

"No I will not come in!" Mr Shelley snapped angrily. "If I wanted to visit foreigners, I'd go abroad."

Mrs Chopra eyes widened in surprise.

"How can I help you then?" Mrs Chopra asked politely.

"Help me?" the old man shrieked. "You can help me by keeping that racket down. Any more of that dreadful wailing and I'll have the police around."

Without waiting to discuss the matter any further, Mr Shelley stalked back next door.

"Well!" gasped Mrs Chopra. "I think that we have upset our new neighbour." She turned to Reeta.

"Perhaps you'd better practise a little more quietly. I don't think that Mr Shelley likes music."

Reeta returned to her sitar. How could she practise quietly when she hadn't been playing loudly in the first place? Her thumbs strummed the first vibrant chords and at that moment an explosion of noise came through the wall.

An enormous black cloud came crashing down the chimney putting out the fire and covering everything in the room with a thick coating of soot.

"AARGH!" They all jumped with surprise. Vijay bent over coughing and spluttering loudly. Then the inevitable happened. The pounding on the front door began again. Mr Chopra opened it this time. On the step was a dusty figure, coal black from top to toe, except for the luminous whites of his blazing eyes.

"How dare you!" Mr Shelley thundered.

"I'm so sorry," Mr Chopra apologised, struggling to control a grin. "I don't know what happened."

"I'll tell you exactly what happened," Mr Shelley exploded, "your chimney needs cleaning!"

"Of course," Mr Chopra suddenly understood, "so when I lit the fire the heat shifted all the soot!"

The old man, covered in dust, looked so funny that Mr Chopra wanted to laugh.

"It looks like your chimney needs cleaning too, Mr Shelley," he grinned.

"It most certainly does not," Mr Shelley replied.

He narrowed his eyes fiercely under his craggy brows,

"That–is–not–my–soot. It–is–your–soot–from–your–chimney," he explained slowly as though he were talking to a five-year-old.

"You will pay for this. I'll have my whole house cleaned and I shall send you the bill!"

With that, the enraged old man stormed off home.

Later, Reeta gazed out of her bedroom. The rain streaked relentlessly down the window but even so, she could make out the hunched figure in the next door garden bent over his precious plants.

"What a pity he is so horrid," Reeta thought with a sigh. "He is such a wizard in the garden, I would love to be able to grow things the way he does. I wonder why he is so nasty... perhaps he is lonely?"

Like most Hindu families cleansing their homes before Diwali, Mrs Chopra was busy with preparations inside the house. She had sent Mr Chopra out to buy the sweets for the festival. Reeta and Vijay escaped to the garden to keep out of the way.

They had not been out for long when the noise began. Reeta shushed her brother and stopped to listen. There it was again, it was definitely a low moaning noise.

"It's just the wind in old misery gut's apple trees," Vijay said.

The moaning sound came again, but this time it was louder. Reeta stopped in her tracks.

"It's coming from next door," she whispered. "And I don't think it is the wind."

"Perhaps he's got a ghost," Vijay shivered.

The noise sounded again, followed this time by a faint cry of

"Help!"

Reeta and Vijay looked at each other.

"Perhaps he has kidnapped somebody and tied them up in there while he holds them to ransom," Vijay whispered fearfully.

"Vijay, stop it!"

"Ahhhhrrrr..." There it was again.

The children could picture someone being held prisoner.

"We have to rescue them," Reeta decided.

"How?" Vijay asked, suddenly afraid.

But Reeta was already half way up the shed and levering herself onto the roof.

"Come on," she beckoned, "we'll creep in from the back."

"He might catch us and take us prisoner too." A hard knot of fear began to form in Vijay's stomach.

"You're not scared are you?"

"No...it's just that..."

"Come on then."

Both children landed on the soil with a soft thud and crouched low behind the leaves of a large plant. Stealthily, Reeta and Vijay crept from plant to bush up the garden. Reeta almost forgot their mission as she breathed in the scent of the chrysanthemums all around her.

They reached the grimy windows and peered cautiously inside, through glass which looked as though it hadn't been cleaned for years.

The room was very untidy and littered with books and newspapers. Mr Shelley was nowhere in sight.

"Perhaps he's gone to pick up the ransom money," whispered Vijay.

Just then the moan came again, this time louder and definitely from somewhere inside the house. Reeta walked boldly up the steps to the faded green back door and bravely turned the handle. The door creaked open and Reeta stepped inside.

The kitchen was exactly the same shape as her own, but more old-fashioned. Reeta wasn't surprised by this. What did take her aback, though, was the smell. The house smelt dusty and cold, so cold that for a while Reeta's nose hurt. She frowned as she saw that the kitchen cupboards were covered in a fine layer of black dust. Mr Shelley hadn't cleaned up very well after the soot fall, despite his threats of huge cleaning bills.

Tiptoeing quietly through the kitchen, Reeta opened the door. At the end of the hall she discovered the source of the noise. Mr Shelley was sprawled in a twisted heap at the bottom of the stairs.

"Oh thank goodness you've come!" he breathed. "My leg... I think it's broken."

"Vijay!" Reeta called.

The little boy appeared at the kitchen door.

"Vijay, go and tell Mummy to call an ambulance and then to come round here. I'll open the front door for her."

The little boy darted off and Reeta turned to Mr Shelley.

"What happened?" she asked.

"I... I fell," he said slowly, trying to sit upright. It was too difficult and a look of pain twisted his face.

"Last night..." he muttered, "...I've been here all night. I couldn't move... to reach the telephone."

Reeta saw that the old man was trembling so she ran upstairs and brought back a pillow and a blanket. Mr Shelley's normally red and angry face was now ashen-grey. As Reeta tucked the blanket around his shoulders, she realised how old and frail he was.

"Would you like a drink?" she asked, after an uncomfortably long silence. Mr Shelley nodded, his eyes closed with exhaustion.

In the kitchen, Reeta was trying to wash up a glass in the icy tap water when her mother and Vijay arrived. Mrs Chopra took charge of the situation and ordered Mr Shelley not to move. She lifted him slightly so that he could sip some of the water that Reeta brought. Just then, the ambulance arrived. The kindly ambulance woman put a temporary splint onto Mr Shelley's leg to keep it steady in case it was broken. It was all too much for him, and as he was being lifted onto the stretcher, he fainted.

That afternoon, Reeta took a bunch of chrysanthemums to the hospital. She found Mr Shelley resting on his bed, his knee heavily bandaged. The old man smiled at the flowers.

"My favourite," he said. "How did you guess?"

"Well..." Reeta answered shyly, "you grow so many of them in your garden that I thought you must like them."

"My word! You noticed that did you?"

Reeta touched the blooms gently. "The yellow ones remind me of the sun."

"Do you like gardening then?" Mr Shelley asked.

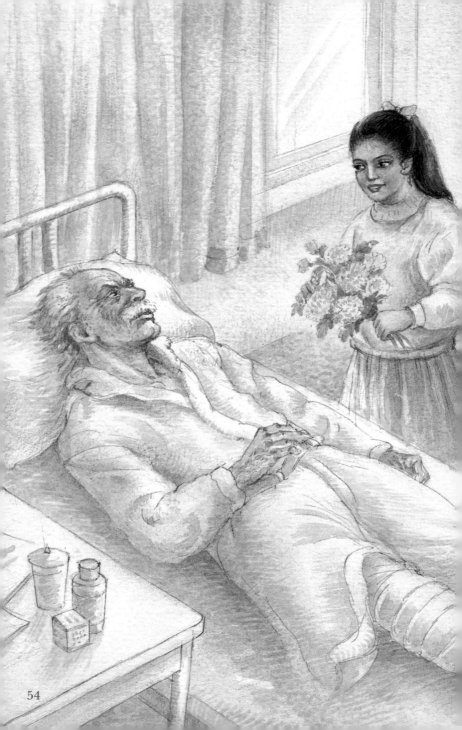

"Oh yes, very much," cried Reeta, launching into her favourite subject.

"My leg isn't broken after all and so I'll be leaving here tomorrow, but do you think that you could check my plants for me this afternoon? I've never left them on their own before, you see."

"Of course I will, Mr Shelley," Reeta said with delight. "It will be a pleasure."

Mr Shelley looked different somehow in his hospital bed, less angry, less frightening. Now, he reminded Reeta of her own Dada back in India. As Reeta put on her coat to leave, Mr Shelley looked up at her. He smiled, embarrassed.

"I... er... I... um," he faltered humbly. "I wanted to thank you for rescuing me – especially after the way I behaved to you."

"It doesn't matter," Reeta smiled.

After their prayers at the temple on Sunday, the Chopras rushed home. They had plenty to do. For one thing, their relatives would be calling around for the Diwali meal and the food had to be prepared and, for another thing, Mr Shelley was expected home.

Reeta watched anxiously from the candle-lit window. It was late in the afternoon by the time the ambulance finally arrived. All the Chopras went outside to help. Mr Shelley, walking awkwardly and leaning on Mr Chopra, went inside and gasped in amazement. His house was clean and sparkling.

Mr Shelley's mouth opened and closed like a goldfish before he was able to utter a few astonished words.

"My word!... I mean who..?"

"We all helped," Reeta explained.

"You shouldn't have..."

"Nonsense," Mr Chopra chipped in briskly. "The mess was mostly our soot anyway. And if neighbours can't help each other in emergencies then what's the point of having them?"

"It is Diwali," Mr Chopra added. "We traditionally clean right through our houses so we simply carried on and did yours as well."

Mr Shelley was overcome with emotion as he gazed around his freshly cleaned living room.

"I don't know how to thank you... you've been so kind."

"Well, you can start by coming for dinner this evening."

"Do you really want a stuffy old man like me around? I'm not very good company," Mr Shelley confessed.

"Of course we do," said Reeta. "My grandfather doesn't live in this country, but Aunty Minal is coming. She's very old so you can talk to her."

"Reeta!" Mrs Chopra scolded, "you mustn't say things like that to your elders."

That evening Mr Shelley arrived bearing an armful of fruits and flowers for the Chopras from his garden. He was immediately settled down in the best armchair which was surrounded by specks of tiny lights from the hundreds of candles dotted all over the room.

"It's pretty," marvelled Mr Shelley, "like Fairyland."

"Diwali is our festival of light," Mr Chopra explained. "We remember the time when the god Rama returned to claim his rightful kingdom."

Mr Shelley shook his head.

"I never was much of a church-goer myself so I don't know much about religion."

This made everyone laugh.

Reeta and Vijay helped to carry great, steaming bowls of curry, potatoes and parathas to the crowded table. Mr Shelley's nose wrinkled suspiciously as the food was offered to him.

"I've never had foreign food before," he said.

"Oh but please try it," Reeta urged.

Seeing his little friend's saucer-like eyes silently pleading with him, Mr Shelley dipped the spoon into the dish and helped himself to a tiny portion. Cautiously he stuck his finger in the juices and put it to his lips.

"Ummm," he said. "Not bad."

He helped himself to three larger spoonfuls.

"I thought that it would have been hot."

"No," laughed Aunty Minal. "Not all dishes have lots of chillies in them. This one is a 'korma', that means 'mild', and much of the flavouring is from different spices."

After that there was no stopping Mr Shelley; he wolfed down two helpings of everything as though he hadn't been fed for a week.

Then he demolished a dish of syrupy *gulab jamons**.

**gulab jamons*: milk sweets in syrup

Licking his lips, Mr Shelley sat back appreciatively.

"That was delicious. I might even try an Indian take-away now."

"There's no need for that," laughed Mrs Chopra. "When we are cooking we will put a little aside for you. Reeta can bring it around."

"And you can use fresh vegetables for your cooking from my garden anytime, just help yourselves."

"Now then Mr Shelley," said Mr Chopra getting up from the table. "Would you like to join us? We are going to do puja."

Mr Shelley looked puzzled.

"It means a prayer ceremony," explained Reeta. "At Diwali a prayer to the goddess Lakshmi asking her for good fortune and prosperity in the year to come."

"Does that include prosperity in the garden?" asked Mr Shelley.

"Why of course," laughed Reeta.

"Well then I'd be delighted to join you."

This book is part of
THE LONGMAN BOOK PROJECT

General Editor Sue Palmer
Fiction Editor Wendy Body
Non-fiction Editor Bobbie Neate

PEARSON EDUCATION LIMITED
Edinburgh Gate, Harlow, Essex, CM20 2JE, England
and Associated Companies throughout the World.

Text © Lisa Dass 1994
Illustrations © Mrinal Mitra 1994
The right of Lisa Dass to be identified as the author of this Work has been asserted
by her in accordance with the Copyright, Designs and Patents Act, 1988.

First published 1994
ISBN 0 582 12216 3
Sixth impression 1999

Printed in Singapore (JBW)

The publisher's policy is to use paper manufactured from sustainable forests.